MW01251915

In Places of Kinship and Animosity:

A Collection of Short Stories

By Randall C. Moss

Contents

For my wife, Ashley

Her stubbornness is the reason my stubbornness
has not yet killed me.

A Foreword

Six years ago, I was told that I had cancer. I was told that it was really aggressive and that I would have to immediately begin my struggle with treatment if I wanted to survive. It took about a week to reflect on the weight of being told something like that and I'm not sure if it ever really processes.

This was the point where I decided I'd write this collection of stories. I thought, or really hoped, that creating characters with their own problems would help me to understand my own situation better. While all of the characters were going to have dreams and particular views of the world, philosophical or otherwise, they were going to be placed in a survival mode where none of that mattered.

Finding energy to write this back then became very problematic, hence the reason for taking so long. This extra time turned out to be a really good thing however, as I gained the advantage of hindsight while writing these stories and I discovered that even in survival mode, people seem to find or long to find a semblance of balance in their worlds.

As you will soon discover, I did write these stories with characters in situations that they never wanted to be in. There are elements of drama, comedy, and horror in these stories. But more than that, these stories are about the connections between people. Maybe it's instinctual, but I found that when I was in survival mode, connecting with someone felt like a necessity.

Well, I'm not much for long introductions, so I would just like to say that I hope you enjoy these stories as much as I have enjoyed writing them.

Randall C. Moss
2020

A Quality of Fear

On a Tuesday night nearing the end of August, Frances Grant laid in her bed alone for the first time in twelve years. Twelve years prior, she had acquired a best friend in a puppy named Mikey. Mikey was a German Shepherd named after Saint Michael. He had aided Frances through both a nasty divorce and a car wreck that left her with a deep scar on her right arm.

Sadly, Mikey had passed away sometime between Monday night and Tuesday morning with the vet just labeling the cause as "old age." Frances was exhausted from the past thirteen hours of sadness. As she lay there, she had momentarily forgotten that Mikey was gone and she reached out for his spot beside her on the bed before drifting off to sleep.

Out of the darkness of her room, she was suddenly startled awake by what sounded like a tapping on a table. Her arm reached for Mikey before she remembered again. Through blurry eyes, she strained to see the time from her clock on the nightstand. It was 3:26 am. She realized that just a few nights ago, she would have startled her boy and he would have at least huffed and readjusted. She had never felt as alone as she did in that moment.

As Frances closed her eyes again, the tapping began again. "Go back to sleep Frances. It's just the witching hour you're hearing," she told herself.

Her mind wandered on the upcoming day. Her mind wandered on something funny that some kid had said in her elementary class one time. And her mind wandered on Mikey.

She thought about the time her mother took her to see Dr. Snake Belly to get a root to help her sleep through the night and she wished she had a root like that now. Dr. Snake Belly was a doctor of voodoo that her mother insisted on taking her to as a child. Frances never put stock in those things as an adult until moments like this in the dark.

As the aloneness was setting back in, she began to feel a little unnerved. It was as though someone or something was watching her. She felt the malice of demon eyes scanning over her and she covered up for protection.

The covers were sweltering in mid-August, but that did not stop her from being completely submersed in them. The image of a hand coming up from under the bed started to pop up in her mind.

"This is ridiculous," she said to herself as she got up and turned the light on.

She checked under her bed for good measure and gave the room a good scan before turning off the lights and getting back into bed. Shortly after getting back into bed again, that feeling started to roll back over her. Then the tapping started again.

"Damnit," she thought to herself when she realized that she had been so intent on checking for monsters that she didn't even inspect for the noise.

The thought of vampires, goblins, and aliens began to go through her mind. The thought of how Mikey made her feel safe when he was around went through her mind. But mostly, the dominant thought that she was having was how she wished she could fall sleep and escape that fear and sadness.

She wondered if maybe she had been hexed. After all, she did burn quite a few bridges with the family of her ex-husband before their divorce finalized. The noise began a pattern of short taps and long silences. In the silences, she would wonder if the noise was all in her head.

Everything began bubbling up inside her and she began to laugh as tears rolled down her face. Frances jumped back up out of bed and turned the lights on again. It was now her mission to find the tapping. She turned over dirty laundry and trinkets and lotions on her vanity, but could not find the source of the noise.

Then she closed her eyes to focus, but the sound of her heartbeat was louder than the room. In defeat, she exhaled and put her head down. The tapping began again as she lifted her head and noticed her vent on the wall.

Frances had a handmade doll made to look like her hanging from the vent on her wall. The doll had spun around to where its face was pressed up against the vent and its button eyes were tapping the vent every time a draft came through. Relief washed over Frances. She knew she would now be able to sleep. The time was 4:02 am when she turned off the lights and covered up knowing she was safe.

After falling into a deep sleep, a brown recluse crawled along her head and down her neck. When she tried to roll over, the spider bit her on the neck. Frances Grant would blame hexes and find metaphors in why these things would happen, but the explanations that she would find would never quite fit the circumstances and her past would always seem happier to her than her present.

A Buckruh Boy's First Love

Levi Armstrong had fallen in love with a girl back in 1935. He was only ten years old back then so to him, the memories of that time would feel as though they were from someone else's life. He had seen her walking home from school a few times before they had actually met but before then, she was just another person to ignore, like background noise on a sidewalk.

On the day that he had fallen in love, his mom had decided to take him and his friend Benny Martin to a place called The Bar-B-Q Shack, just outside of town. For them, this was the modern equivalent to going to a theme park. The Bar-B-Q Shack was really just a pit in the ground with a pig roasting over it and a wooden slant that covered a makeshift counter in front of the pit.

Levi's mother would stand in line for barbeque listening to gossip about the town folk that she couldn't hear anywhere else. Then she would walk a few houses down and have her hair done up. The part Levi and Benny were really excited about was that they had always seen a bunch of older kids out by the pit playing a game called *King of the Mountain*. The object of this game was to get to the top of the hill and declare yourself king while everyone else tried to knock you off the "mountain." They had always wanted to stop and play.

Benny had been even more thrilled than Levi. Benny's dad had gone into one of his bad moods and started taking it out on him on that day. Fourteen years earlier, Benny's dad had made a small fortune selling watered down shine to closet alcoholics that didn't know any better during the initial years of prohibition. His dad would eventually piss away all of his money before shooting himself when Benny would turn eighteen. That's when Benny would join the army. But on this day, young Benny just wanted to get away from a brand of blame and guilt that he was not equipped to understand.

When their car pulled up to the pit, the smell of barbeque was overwhelming and their mouths fell into a constant state of watering. The smoke was so strong that mosquitoes and flies were not even swarming in the air. A usual group of grown-ups had congregated around the spit. The kids Levi and Benny were looking for had not yet come out to play, however. Nonetheless, they ran to the hill to play their game.

"I am king of this mountain, I am king of the world!" said Benny as he balled up his fists and put them on his hips.

"Now I am," said Levi as he caught Benny off guard and pushed him off his perch.

"Oh no, I've been dethroned!" declared Benny. He put his shoulder down and ran back up the hill and hit Levi so hard that he did not have time to prepare for the roll down the hill.

Levi laid there at the bottom of that hill with his head pointed to the sky and his eyes closed, taking in all of the joy and pain of his childhood. When he opened his eyes, he saw a young girl in a pink plaid dress walking his way. He knew he had seen her before, but in that moment, she was the most beautiful thing that he had ever seen.

She held out her arm to help him up. "You're not very good at this game are you?" she asked with a smile and a strong southern accent. Levi tried to retort, but nothing came out.

"I'm Alma," she said. "Can I play with y'all? I'll show you how it's done."

Benny, Alma and Levi played for a while until the older kids showed up and overtook the hill. Benny refused to admit that the older kids were too rough for them, so he continued playing. Alma and Levi sat side by side on the ground watching him try.

"When you become king of the world one day, can I be the queen?" asked Alma sitting there in the clay with a voice that made Levi's heart jump.

"I wouldn't have it any other way," Levi assured her in the most suave way that a ten year old could. She put her head on his shoulder and they sat there in the silence for eons. Suddenly, Alma jumped up and ran straight up the hill at full speed. She grabbed the boy that had been standing at the top unmovable and they both fell off the hill.

"Now," she yelled out to Levi, "Run to the top." Benny saw what was going on and tripped another kid from running up the hill. It took a second, but Levi finally broke from a mix of astonishment and bewilderment, and began running.

"I am king of the mountain!" he proclaimed as he looked over at Alma. "And Alma is my queen!" Another one of the older kids hit him from behind, knocking him off as soon as he got those words out of his mouth. When he hit the ground, he and Alma looked at each other and began laughing.

Benny continued playing with those older kids as if he had something to prove. Levi and Alma continued to watch him and they rooted for him every time he started up the hill. At some point Levi and Alma began holding hands.

After a while, the inevitable happened. "Hell no! Alma, get your dirty ass away from there. You don't do that with some buckruh boy. Come eat your bittle," shouted a lady that had ventured out from the pit to see what the kids were doing.

From the tone of the lady's voice, anyone could've picked up on the fact that she was madder than hell. The lady was Alma's mother. When Alma went to her mother, she received a hard pop on her leg for having sinned in such a way. Levi wondered then if he would ever see her again.

After that day, Levi would see her, but only from across some street or from the other side of a fence. Later, he would see her as a proud young woman in the middle of a demonstrating crowd. Still later, he would see her with possibly her grandchildren at a city park. He never spoke to her again, but he would always wonder if she remembered the day she turned a lovesick buckruh boy into a king.

A Hierarchy of Pain

The dawn was brought in through squinted eyes on that tragic day. Most of the fishermen had slept late and were just waking up as the horizon was coming into focus. They had had a long night of celebrating their huge bounty of the day before and were just coming out of their rum and whisky naps with quiet smirks. As they woke, the young men skipped along the path to the ocean, aiding the old fools amid the trudging.

Watching the routine of these men was a young boy selling bait for part-time fishermen by the shore. His name was Alon and he dreamed of one day becoming one of these men going out on their fishing boats. He was a small, skinny kid with a dirty shirt and a stomach that growled louder than a dog barks. Every day, Alon would wake up just before the fishermen and cast his net in waist-high water for bait fish. On good days he could sell enough bait to get some bread and some fruit for his family. On bad days he would go hungry.

On this day, he was starving. The day before would have been one of the best days for selling bait had he not been robbed by an older man with a machete. The man had pulled the knife on Alon as he was heading back to his hut. When Alon handed the money over to the man, he wept like a baby. The man made a cut Alon's palm with the machete as his way of showing Alon that it could have been worse. He could have been chopped up.

When Alon got home, he was pouring blood from his hand and tears from his eyes. He felt like a failure to his family. His mother bandaged him up and let him cry out his emotions before trying to comfort him.

"Being robbed is not so bad. It could be worse," she said. "At least you're not one of those kids that are forced to work in the mines or the cane fields. At least you didn't lose your hand. At least you're not one of those bait fish that you sell. There are a lot of people and creatures that have it worse than you."

Alon's stomach growled as he thought of these things from the day before. He was hungry enough to eat one of his bait fish raw, but he didn't. He did not want to chance it that that one fish being sold would be the difference between having enough money for bread and not having enough. He smiled as he watched the fishermen board their boats and he began to feel dizzy.

He thought about kids that had it a lot worse than he did. He wondered what they thought about to pacify themselves since they had it the worst. In a weird way, Alon envied those kids because at least they could feel bad about their situation and not feel guilty about feeling that way. He wondered exactly where the line was drawn where he could feel bad about himself without feeling guilty about it.

The morning had grown overcast quickly as the last fishing boat left the shore. Alon reached to pick up his bait bucket with his bandaged hand before realizing it and grabbing it with his other hand. He started for the path away from the beach but in that moment, he felt water on his feet. A large wave had hit the beach and brought the tide in further than usual. The sky became ominous in an instant. Alon ran to the edge of the path that led back to his hut.

As he reached the start of the path, the earth growled a growl louder than his stomach. When he turned to look, he saw a wave larger than the sky. He knew that there was no escape from the wave. He would be swallowed by the ocean. It was in that moment that it did not matter that he did not work in a mine or a cane field. It did not matter that he wasn't a bait fish. It was in that moment that suffering was suffering and the end result would all be the same.

The Jumper and the Werewolf

Have you ever thought about an event or a situation from your past and wished you could remember it differently? I'm not talking about anything actually changing. I'm just talking about remembering an event or situation in a different way. I'm just talking about remembering it in a way that the butterfly flapping its wings across the other side of the world doesn't ruin some poor soul here in this reality. If that makes sense to you, that wish, or feeling that comes from that wish, is what the night was like when I met Will.

I couldn't sleep that night and decided to go for a walk. I had stepped out of my apartment in the city and began walking towards the river. I don't think there was any intuition involved in this decision. It was just dumb bad luck. The city was soggy wet. The road was like a Christmas tree amid all the drizzling streetlights and a bright half-moon of a waterlogged night.

And so I walked. God so help me, I walked a good four blocks without even realizing it. It was a weird feeling, that walk. It was some kind of insomniac trance or something, but I got all the way to the river before I realized it. As I stood there on the bank, I took a deep sigh and looked up at the Maheegan Bridge. There was something up there. It was just a person I was sure, but it looked like a creature doing cartoon-like, burglar tip-toe steps to the arc of the bridge. I decided to go up on the bridge myself to get a better look. Had I known then what I know now, maybe everything would've changed. But I don't want that. I just wish I could remember it differently.

The Maheegan Bridge is a steep bridge. It's the type of bridge that runners only attempt when they are trying to punish themselves. That night, the bridge had winded me at about twenty seconds into the climb. As I looked ahead, the light bouncing off the wetness around it obscured the figure I was trying to make out until I was almost upon it. My heavy breathing didn't help either. Once I was able to see that it was just a man, I was a little disappointed. I mean, I knew that it would be, but something about it was still disappointing.

The man was small and skinny. He looked a little sickly and he had his arms crossed in a way that looked like he was holding or consoling himself. His hair was disheveled and greasy, but that seemed to be the norm in the city. With all of his flaws, he gave me the impression of a good person that wasn't going to try and hustle or rob me. And if he was a druggy, he wasn't a seasoned druggy. He was staring at the water going under the bridge as if it contained the secret to life.

"Good evening," I said to him. "Whatcha doing out here tonight?" The man didn't look up or acknowledge that he heard me. In the awkward silence, I talked even more. "As for me, I couldn't sleep. I walked and I walked and I was up this damn bridge before I even knew it. And now I can't make heads or tails of why I came up here in the first place. I think I am at my stupidest when I can't sleep." There was another long moment of nothing from Mr. Chatty before I decided to cut my losses and walk away. "Okay then, I'll be seeing you," I said.

"My name's Will," said the man just after I turned my back to walk away.

"Hey Will, I'm Tully," I responded as I turned back around and stuck out my hand for a handshake. The sickly little man shook my hand in the most awkward way possible. It couldn't have been any more awkward if he had gone in for a hug. His hands were clammy and soft, like a warm wet sock.

"Okay, well, it was nice to meet you," said Will, hinting that he wanted this little exchange to be over.

"It was nice to meet you too, Will," I replied as I gave him a little head nod and turned to walk away.

"I'm going to jump off this bridge," he said matter-of-factly. I turned back around and gave him the look of someone that had just misheard something. "I am only telling you this so that you won't blame yourself if you read about it in the paper and wonder if there was something you did or could've done. I want you to know that I am going to do this and there is nothing that can be done that will stop this."

How does a person respond to something like that? How should a person respond to that? The answer to that is something that I still do not know. On that night, I mumbled out the only phrase I could think of to say. "Don't do that."

"It's too late, my friend. It's gonna happen. But it's for the best."

I reached in my pocket for my phone. If I called the police, I thought maybe I could restrain him till they got there. Alas, I had left my phone at the apartment and the only things I had to grab were keys and pocket lint. "Why would you do that? Did a girlfriend leave you? A boyfriend, maybe? Let me tell you, it's going to get better."

Will laughed. It was a good, loud, hearty laugh. "I wish it were something that simple. But people have died by my actions. By my hands. And it's not fair to continually risk that happening again."

"Is that true, Will? Have you murdered someone?" The sickly man was wringing his hands at this point. The weight of that question seemed to be eating him alive.

"Maybe, but it's not like you think. You see, I'm a. I'm a. I'm a werewolf." Now I thought I had misheard the thing about jumping off the bridge, but I thought I knew for sure that I had misheard this.

"You're not a werewolf." I knew it wasn't the most subtle thing to say at the time, but I had blurted it out before I knew I had said it. We probably all have delusions to some degree, but this one was a doozy. "What makes you think you're a werewolf?" Everything that was coming out of my mouth now felt abrasive and wrong, but I didn't know what to say or how to act. All I wanted was to take a walk and I had suddenly become a psychiatrist for a man trying to commit suicide. It was a little bit much.

"Did you hear about the mutilated couple in the park? Did you hear about the postal worker that had his spleen ripped out on 84th Street about three weeks ago?" I did not respond because I had heard of both of these incidents. The couple in the park was one of the very reasons I couldn't sleep that night. I had stumbled upon the crime scene the morning after it happened. The police had just put the caution tape up, but had not had a chance to cover anything. It was beautiful in its chaos, but it was awful.

"Well, I certainly heard about them. I more than heard about them," he continued. "The day after these events, I didn't understand why I woke up naked beside the dumpster outside my building, covered in red paint. After a shower, I listened to the news and I knew. I just knew. The moon is in its first quarter tonight and I'm not waiting around again for something bad to happen."

"Do you remember doing those things?" I asked.

"No, but I know I did them. I can feel the evil of those deeds pulsing through me. I can feel that evil asking

29

for more and I know that in about a week, I won't be able to control it."

"How did you become a werewolf, then?"

"It was this dream I had. At least I thought it was a dream, but it must not have been. I was walking down one of those trails up in the hills. I was whistling something when I came across this big, glowing pair of yellow eyes. I tried to say something like 'good doggy' but nothing came out. The yellow eyes leaped forward and that's all I remember. I woke up covered in sweat and what looked like red paint, but no visible marks on me where I had been bitten or injured."

"Wouldn't you have a bite mark if you were bitten, though?"

"Look, I don't know how this works either. All I know is that, from that point on, I've had these urges. These feelings. I don't want them, but I know I can't control them forever."

"But isn't it possible that that was a dream? Don't you think that you could be getting worked up for nothing?"

"It's possible, I guess. But I haven't found any proof that what this is could be anything else. I know it. In my heart, I know it. There is an evil clashing inside me with everything that's not a werewolf. The werewolf will overtake me again. I know it."

I thought about what he was saying for a moment. I thought about the word, proof. I thought about the crime scene of the mutilated couple. And then I realized something. "Will, I came upon the crime scene at the park the morning after it happened. The police didn't release much information, but I watched one of the officers pick up a knife and put it in an evidence bag. Werewolves don't use knives. You can't be a werewolf, Will! There was a knife used at the crime scene!"

His eyes deadened a little. "Are you sure?" he asked. I nodded. "Maybe, maybe I'm not a werewolf, then." I couldn't tell if he believed himself as he said this. I couldn't tell if he believed me about the knife. "Maybe I'm just a regular person. Oh my God, that's even worse. If I'm not a werewolf and I did those things..." He broke off into a mumble. I couldn't understand the mumble, but I think he was coming to terms with a new reality.

"What are you doing? Will, get down! Will, don't jump. No, no, no. Please don't. Will!" It was too late. He jumped. He was right. There was nothing I could do.

The police would search for Will's body along the banks and further down the river, but it was never found. The things that must've been going through his mind when he jumped haunt me every day. Sometimes the monsters that we are in reality are worse than the ones that we think we are. Will was neither of those monsters, however. The killer of the couple in the park and the postal worker on his route was apprehended a week later. He gave his full confession.

Looking back at this incident now, I wish I could remember it differently. I wish he were the killer and not just a man trying to escape his own delusions. I wish I could give him that. The crazy thing is I've been having strange dreams lately in this prison cell involving dried, red paint. Maybe it's just left over trauma from the situation. But maybe that's how werewolves infect you. Instead of a bite, maybe it's just a transfer of mental hell from one person to another. And if that's the case, maybe there are more werewolves out there than we think.

Cow Tipping

Emma Cassidy sat in the back of Mr. Navarre's eleventh grade science class thinking about everything but schoolwork, but mostly she thought about Tommy Carter. Tommy was all business in school, with the exception of a few sly smiles and funny faces made to Emma from the front of the classroom. She and Tommy had been best friends since they were nine years old playing at a local park on the merry-go-round. She thought about that merry-go-round every single day.

When the bell rang, Emma and Tommy met up to wait for Perry Boatwright behind the school. Perry was Tommy's best guy friend and, for Emma, was the most tolerable third wheel that she and Tommy could have had.

"I can't stay long today, Emma. I told my mom I had a meeting with a World Improvement Club to discuss how children are starving in other countries while American kids don't even finish their meals. She loves when I use an excuse that somehow puts us down at the same time," Tommy grinned. His grin seemed to be that of genuine hate toward his mother. Emma should've seen some kind of red flag in that, but hind sight is twenty-twenty.

When Perry arrived, he explained that he had a new vendetta against a kid named Petey Dothan. Perry told them that he heard this asshole say that Emma had given him and most of the twelfth grade class a blow job behind the cafeteria and that she must have deserved growing up without a father because of her transgressions. Emma was used to the small town bullshit that comes from the rumor mill, but she knew that the real vendetta probably had to do with something Petey said or did to Perry. This did not change the fact that she would still be on board with whatever they were going to do to humiliate this Petey kid.

You see, this Petey Dothan kid was an up and coming football player and typical good ole boy. He lived in the town of Hilliard all of his life just like Emma, Tommy and Perry. The difference between them and Petey, though, was that no one looked down on Petey because he was poor. His mother never got busted for selling drugs. His father never left him on his birthday as a child. And none of his family members ever got shot after getting drafted into a war that they had no choice over. He was from a bible thumper family that secretly believed that good fortune meant good standing with God (though they would never admit this). Petey never knew what it was to be viewed by the entire town as children that will never amount to anything.

Perry's big plan was to take Petey snipe hunting, but everyone and their brother had already heard of snipe hunting, so Emma suggested cow tipping. Their plan, of course, had to be more complicated than just taking Petey cow tipping. Whether it would be incriminating pictures or a good old fashion rumor was uncertain, but they would figure out the details later.   The first step was getting him to comply so later on, Emma walked up to the asshole in question with a friendly grin and a pat on the back.

"Petey! How are you doing?" she said in the best concerned voice she could muster.

"What in the hell do you want, Emma Cassidy?" he asked with a hint of disdain. He had always thought Emma was pretty, but he was no fool. He could feel the hate and divide among their cliques.

"Well, you know Perry and Tommy? We were planning on going cow tipping tonight, but we need a fourth. You're the strongest guy we know, so I thought I'd ask you."

"You guys are idiots. You can't tip cows. They're too big," he proclaimed smugly. He really was a cocky bastard.

"Sure you can," Emma told him. "I'll show you tonight."

"Whatever. I have nothing better to do. I'll watch y'all make fools of yourselves," he replied. The trap was set.

That night, Emma and her mom were sitting down on the couch in their trailer just before Emma was set to leave out to meet Tommy and Perry. Their trailer was a small single wide that they had lived in since she was born. It was on land that had still been in the name of Emma's

35

grandfather on her father's side and they just paid the bills as though they were coming in the mail in her mother's name. It was just an acre of land, but she could never understand how her father could just leave his family and his land. Her father left out of embarrassment for being crippled by a machinery incident at the packing plant when she turned eight years old. Her mom never told her exactly what happened to her father. She would just get very emotional and tell her that one day she could ask him about it.

They ate fried bologna sandwiches and watched an infomercial about some machine that made spaghetti. Emma's mom looked less stressed than she had looked in weeks and Emma was tempted to stay home and enjoy those good times with her mom while she still could. It's a hard thing for a teenager to think about mortality, so Emma would always shrug off those feelings as if she had infinite days with her mother. If only she had listened to her initial instinct back then.

"How are you really doing, Emma? Did you tell Tommy how you feel yet?" probed her mother. She had always known how Emma felt about Tommy since the car ride home from the park with that merry-go-round when they were nine years old. The thing with her mom was that she could always ask things like that without seeming like a nosy parent to a teenager. It was truly a gift.

"No mom. I just can't do it right now. What if he doesn't feel the same way? Maybe someday when I'm famous, I'll be able to," Emma replied back.

"Just know that things never happen as you plan them, Em," her mom tried to sound as profound as she could. "He's not going to wait around on you forever." With a knowing nod to her mother, Emma left the trailer to meet Tommy and Perry.

Petey Dothan would never show up that night. Emma's mother died of a brain aneurism shortly after the infomercial ended. Tommy never knew how Emma felt and Emma never knew that she would be Tommy's greatest regret. Regret and the grief of that night would always be in Emma's peripheral for the rest of her life.

Murder of Monsters

Hector Granum closed his eyes, gripped his shovel tight with his callused hands and, for the third time that day, swung as hard as he could, making solid contact with the left temple of the corpse of old Mrs. Karlov. He felt a slight give in his swing, as though it were the last chop in taking down an old oak tree. In the moment, he was not thinking of the morbid consequences of these actions. Fear and instinct for survival were his only motivations.

Two hours earlier, Hector's world was as anyone may have imagined it. It was morning. His wife, Lydia had already left for work. He was making toast. He was worrying about what the traffic for that day would bring. He was listening to the morning news blaring from the TV from another room. Two hours earlier, there was no fear for his life from a mass of lifeless monsters that vaguely resembled the people of days past.

At the start of the nightmare he was now living, an urgent report on the news rang out, like the urgent reports of every other morning, while he was brushing his teeth. The voice of the newscaster went in and out over the sound of running water and the swishes of his toothbrush over his teeth, "...These people are extremely dangerous. There have been over 130 deaths already..." Hector paused for a moment to wonder how close this tragedy was to him. He was guessing that those "dangerous people" must have been some kind of bombers or mad gunmen.

Two minutes later, there was a knock on his door. It wasn't really a knock, though. It sounded more like a thud. Hector turned off the TV. Looking through the peephole, he saw his neighbor, Adam. Adam was a divorcee in his late thirties that tried to dress as though he were trying out for a department store catalog. His grayish-blonde hair was perfectly combed and he always wore some type of golf shirt with a popped collar.

"My man Hector! How you doin'?" he asked as soon as Hector opened the door. He took the sign of the door opening at all as a sign that he should barge in and he stepped right by Hector.

Adam looked a little different, though. His hair was slightly out of place and that was something that just did not happen for this man. "Is it windy outside? I've never seen your hair fall down like that?" asked Hector.

"What the hell you talkin' about?" Adam pulled out his comb to fix whatever strands might have escaped. "How am I now?" he asked once he finished his routine with the comb.

Hector watched that perfect blonde hair fall right back out of place. "Well," said Hector, not really sure if he wanted to continue with this conversation as a second rate mirror to this guy. Then he watched another strand of Adam's hair fall in front of his face. Then a tiny trickle of blood came down from that forest of hair and ran in a soft red trail between his eyes and down the left side of his nose.

"What the hell man!" yelled Hector as he took a step backward. Being creeped out was a mild way to put it.

"What?" asked Adam. But in that moment, the right side of his face started to droop. His left shoulder drooped as well. "Hector, you need to see a agghhhh." Blood began pouring out of his mouth, but he continued to try and speak. The pupil of Adam's left eye shot to the ground as if gravity had knocked it down, but his right eye continued staring right at Hector. He began chomping into the air and dragging his drooping body toward Hector.

"Stop man. Stop. If you – you don't stop, I'm gonna have to." Hector looked around for something to stop him. By his back door there was a shovel. He had brought it in the house to kill a snake that had gotten in a week ago. "Stop man. Please," he pleaded. Hector ran over and grabbed the shovel. He paused for a moment and then took a stance to swing. The monster that Adam had become made one last chomp at the air before Hector resided to the fact that it had really come to this.

He closed his eyes and swung as hard as he could. Hector made solid contact with his neighbor's shoulder, causing him to stumble and trip over an ottoman that he and Lydia had bought on sale a little over a year before. The monster looked up from the ground and began his chomping again. Adam's face was hardly recognizable to Hector. Hector took aim again, closing his eyes just before committing the deed. This time he made contact with the monster's head. The strike was not square. The side of the shovel came down just above Adam's good eye, but the part of the shovel that hit did more than enough damage to silence him.

Murder was all Hector could think about. He turned the TV back on. "These people are infected with a virus. Please keep your distance. At this time, we do not know what the cause of the infection is," shouted the reporter on the special news report. Hector turned the television back off. He'd heard enough. He had watched enough movies to know what this was. This was all too surreal for him.

He locked his doors and sat on the couch staring at the monster corpse that he had murdered. He thought about how odd it was that the body in front of him looked more alive now than it had just moments before. There was a long period of silence. It lasted fifteen, maybe thirty minutes. Finally, curiosity got the better of him and he looked out his window. Walking down the street was another monster of the dead. It looked like it used to be Mrs. Karlov. If it got her, Mr. Karlov was probably already a gonner too. A few moments later, he would be outside swinging at her temple.

Once Mrs. Karlov's concaved skull hit the ground, Hector heard a loud, eardrum piercing shrill from across the street. It came from the lawn of the hermit lady. Everyone called her that because they had never seen her come out of her house. She was standing on her front lawn in horror.

"It's okay. She was a monster," he yelled at the horrified lady. Only as he looked closer, he noticed that blood was trickling from the top of her scalp as well. "Aaaggghhh," was the only reply of the hermit lady across the street. Hector braced himself for another attack. The monster across the street did not take another step forward though, and there was a sort of standoff for a moment.

Darrin and Walter were running from their houses from a block over to investigate the noise. Darrin and Walter were retired army veterans that headed up neighborhood yard sales and block parties in the summer. They were best friends ever since Walter moved into the neighborhood three years back. Darrin was running at first to check out the situation, but his gait turned into a slow, dragging shuffle by the time he got to the middle of the street. Hector stood his ground with his shovel. Walter, who had began as a slow, wobble walk, took a little longer to catch up.

"Watch out, guys. There's monsters," cautioned Hector. "Uhhhggg," was the response from Darrin. Hector was in dismay as he watched Darrin's face droop like Adam's had about an hour ago. When Walter caught up, he realized they were all infected. He was in a standoff with all three monsters. They weren't trying to go after him like in the movies, but they definitely appeared to want to eat him.

"I'll kill every one of you sons of bitches," he yelled. The jaws of the lifeless creatures clamped down hard as their teeth clapped their mouths shut. The sound of their chomping was getting louder and louder. This would be Hector's final standoff.

"Sir, drop the shovel," yelled a voice from behind him. A wave of relief washed over him for a split second to hear a human voice. He didn't even consider what the voice was saying to him. When he turned around, Hector saw two police men with guns drawn. "Sir, I'm not going to tell you again. Drop the aaagggghhh." This thing had gotten the police men and turned them too. He watched the flesh on their faces begin to sag like melting ice cream.

Hector was surrounded on all sides now. He swung the shovel through the air to caution them all to stay back. Suddenly, he felt a jolt of electricity go through his body. He looked down and saw that two barbed darts with wires attached had hit the back of his right calf. As he stared at the entry point, he noticed that his calf had been bitten. There was a bloody chunk taken out and the wires were coming out of that divot. He knew it wouldn't be long now before he'd be another one of the dead masses. Yanking out the darts from his leg, he decided that he wasn't going down without a fight. Hector gripped the shovel tight again and raised it over his head.

"Alright you sons of bitches. Let's do this," he shouted in a shaky voice. In the next moment, he looked around for the best option at getting out and charged hard at the smaller of the two dead police creatures. Three steps in his final charge, he felt a sharp sting in his left thigh and fell. On the fall, the shovel flew out of his hands and landed just short of the monsters in police uniforms. Someone had shot him in the leg. He was done for.

"Arrgghh. Agggghhhh." The voices of the monsters were a unanimous chorus of rotting flesh as the sound of dragging bodies inched closer to him, helpless on the ground. Hector looked around, desperate for a way out. There was no way out. As the horde stood over him, reaching down, Hector passed out.

"We now interrupt your regularly scheduled broadcast for a special news bulletin. The unknown virus that is ravaging the country has now been isolated and a vaccine has been created. Now, thanks to the Highland Center for Neurological Disease, we have learned that the deadly symptoms of the virus should only last about a week. Those that have yet to contract the virus should immediately seek the closest temporary vaccination tent in your area," announced the voice on the radio of an ambulance. "This virus triggers the same parts of your brain that controls perception and, in case you have been lucky enough to have not experienced it first hand, people infected with this virus begin to perceive those around them as, well, perceive them as zombies. I don't know if that's the right terminology, but that is what we have so

44

far. If at all possible, I urge you all. Please do not engage with someone infected with this virus."

One of the EMTs turned the car radio down and turned up the volume of the dispatch radio. "Everything is going to be alright Mr. Granum. We'll just let that nasty virus take its course and go from there," whispered the EMT in a calm, soothing voice. Hector was strapped down to a gurney, unable to move.

"How's he doing?" asked the driver.

"Physically, he'll live. I don't think any of us will get past these next few days mentally."

For the next week, Hector would be handcuffed to a hospital bed, scared to death of the rotted flesh corpses that would come in and out of the room. His wife, Lydia, was infected as well, but she had died jumping out of her car on the freeway trying to make a run for it.

Life tried to go back to before the virus. No one ever discovered how or why the virus began.

A Break from Despondence

Lazarus Heed was a young man in his late twenties. He was painter, both by trade and craft. He would work odd jobs during the off season of exterior house painting, but his dream had always been to be recognized as a proper artist. On a late October day, he was finishing up on repainting the porch railing of a house for a lady named Mrs. Ruth when a deep depression washed over him. As he began folding up a drop cloth to put next to papers, scrapers and cans of paint in a corner of her porch, he stared longingly down the road.

Mrs. Ruth walked outside with a glass of sweet tea in her hand for him. She was a widowed, blue haired lady of her sixties and was a close friend of Lazarus' father before the incident. Lazarus' father had fallen into a fit of depression eleven years back and hung himself from the Woodshire Falls footbridge in the local park. Ever since then, Mrs. Ruth seemed to look at Lazarus with pity. He absolutely hated this, but she was too nice for him to say anything. She had decided to hire him for this job more out of pity than her urge for its necessity.

"Here you go Laz," she said smiling as she handed him the glass of tea.

"Much obliged ma'am," he said, thanking her while sitting down on the porch swing.

He had brought a magazine over to read during breaks so, after a healthy swig, he set down his glass of tea and pulled it out to read while on the porch. The magazine was about art and the headline article read *The Zombification of Painting: How Painting is Dead and is Now Only Feeding Off The Cerebral.* He watched Ruth lip synch the title as an afterthought and he wondered what she might possibly know about any form of art.

"Painting ain't dead Laz. Esther will want you to do her house once she comes over for bridge and sees what kind of work you do. Always a 'keeping up with a Jones'er,' that one," responded Mrs. Ruth in a weird attempt at comfort.

After a short rest on the porch swing, Lazarus felt the urge to paint on canvas, so he left Mrs. Ruth's and walked down to a creek in the woods by a trailer he had been renting. He had begun yet another attempt in trying to paint his masterpiece that would never come. The spot he chose was what he called his "secret squirrely spot." He wasted most of his time out there trying to come up with a reason why he made every single brush stroke. It was what most of the town people would've called a horseshit way to spend an afternoon, but at least it was his horseshit way.

He would do an exercise where he would close his eyes and try to say out loud what it was that he wanted to articulate. "I want to paint outside in the woods because it brings my vision into fruition. This is my method, my construction. I swipe this paint across the canvas on this spot because, because (he hesitated) I don't fucking know." Having conceded, he dropped his head for a less than dramatic sigh.

"How the fuck am I ever going to be a real artist if I can't even explain myself? What the fuck's the point?" he looked up and asked out loud as if he thought the woods were going to answer him. He felt himself sinking deeper into the depression and was unsure how to fight it. His mind kept flashing imagery of his father years ago, just before the bridge incident.

"Hey buddy, you mind shutting your cock sucker for at least fifteen minutes to give the wildlife a rest from your 'me, me' bullshit?" said some son-of-a-bitch from under his hat. The man had been lying nearby, under a tree unnoticed until then. That voice was so familiar to Lazarus that he could hear it in his sleep. It was the voice of Billy Pickett. Billy used to sell Lazarus weed back in high school. They never spoke to each other in terms of serious life issues, but they had bonded in their unfulfilled potential.

"Holy shit, is that William Pickett I see?" Lazarus said back smiling sideways at him on the ground.

"Laz, you know better than to call me by my full name. You can whisper William Pickett in the ear of a stump-broke cow before softly caressing its ears for a ride for all I care, but call me Billy. Listen, I've been up all night sipping mouthwash while trying to convince some cunt of an old lady why vinyl siding is better than traditional wood. I came out here to get away from the thought of what I may or may not have done in the stupor of minty freshness. How about fifteen minutes of peace, huh?" Billy said with a smirk from under his hat.

Lazarus turned his head slightly sideways and looked out the corner of his eyes at Billy. Billy was great for him in the worst of ways, like a big wool security blanket in July. A big shit-eating grin overtook Lazarus' face.

"I don't give a shit about your cow humping sessions. I'm here because it's too fucking hot by the road and I won't go in town because I'm scared I might run into your sister. You finger bang that bitch once and she suddenly thinks that makes her a proper lady. You need to let that bitch know that you Pickett's are stone cold fuck-a-bouts." Lazarus cocked his head downward with perched ears in hopes of a reaction then turned back to the easel. Billy didn't even have a sister, but it was always understood that realities such as that shouldn't get in the way of a good insult.

"Hey, Laz?" said Billy.

"Yeah, Billy?"

"It's good to see you too."

Lazarus was in heaven. His depression would lift, if only for that moment. He smiled again as he threw paint at the canvas on the easel and the two men shared the sacred, noisy quiet of the woods.

The Descent of Margaret Bailey

Margaret Bailey was falling. She had been falling from the sky for the past three hours. It defied all explanations. She could not remember how or why this was happening. When she had awakened three hours ago, her digital watch said Tuesday and her stomach was in her throat.

She had rapidly gone through the emotional stages of impending doom and was now accepting her fate. For the life of her, she could not figure out why she was up there. Clearly, she must've suffered some kind of head injury to not remember. There had to be some kind of plane involved. But wouldn't she have hit the ground by now?

Looking around in the sky, there was no plane in sight. There were no clouds in sight. From the ground, there was no burning from a crash and the little squared plots of land were unrecognizable below her. The ground continued to look as though it were getting closer, but it never seemed to be any closer at the same time. It was as if there was some kind of optical illusion.

Surely she wouldn't have jumped out of a plane without a parachute. Above her was only bright atmosphere that stung her eyes when she looked at it with no cloud cover. Every now and then, she thought she heard a roar and a trickling sound like rain in the distance. With no clouds though, it may have just been the wind rushing through her ears.

She could remember the day before plainly. She had a peanut butter, banana and honey sandwich for breakfast. She visited her mother's grave. And she went to an ATM at a bank and withdrew $1,500 out of her account. Wait, why did she withdraw almost all of her money out? That made no sense. She could not remember.

About an hour earlier, she had searched her clothes for clues. She did find her cell phone, but there was no service. She had been trying desperately to call, text, send an email, and try every kind of social media she had, but nothing went through and nothing pulled up. The fact that she had it with her must've indicated that she was not planning on falling from the sky. She had typed goodbye in a text line and put the phone in her pocket, but now it dawned on her that she didn't look at the pictures on her phone. Maybe she had taken a picture today that would give her some clue.

Taking her phone out again and scrolling through the pictures, she did find two at the end that she didn't remember. One looked to be a blurred image of an ATM machine and the other looked to be a blurred image of a sidewalk and the tip of a man's brown shoe. It must've been accidental photos when she was taking out all of her money. She tried to remember which bank location this was and what this might've meant. She remembered nothing as she heard the rumbling and trickling sounds off in the distance again.

That was her last ditch effort for solving her falling mystery. The mystery fell in line with her emotions on death and she finally accepted that she would never know why the hell she was up there in the first place as well. She put her phone back in her pocket and started to put her legs together and put her arms by her side to make herself a giant bullet. She hoped this would speed up the process of forever falling. "See you soon," she said out loud to the ground.

Just then, her phone beeped. How? She reached for it and saw that it was somehow connected to her daughter, Gabrielle's wireless hotspot. "Where am I?" she texted.

Margaret's phone beeped again. "Where RU?" Gabrielle texted back.

"I'm falling," Margaret texted back to her daughter. There was a pause and then Margaret typed one more thing. "I'm not going to make it." As Margaret finished her text, she looked up from her phone and there was the ground, big as ever. She hit. She only saw it for a split second.

Then there were voices in the background, but no sight. No vision for her.

"What the hell happened out there?"

"Apparently, they caught the Millerton Murderer red handed."

"No shit? How?"

"This lady, Ms. Bailey, was attacked by that piece of shit. He got to her on her way to the ATM and robbed her. Strangled her too, but she didn't die. She was thrown into a makeshift coffin to be buried. The piece of shit took her money, but left the things in her pocket. Somehow in all this, she was trying to use her phone at the exact same time that her daughter was walking by looking for her. Her phone connected to her daughter's phone hotspot right in front of The Ulosvi Cemetery and that's when the daughter flags down Officer Fallon. He walks in the cemetery and stops the son of a bitch right as he's trying to bury her alive."

"That's unreal!"

"Yeah. I don't think she'll ever be the same. I know I wouldn't. Her first words when she was unearthed were, 'I'm not gonna make it.'"

Margaret listened to the two men talking, but she could not respond. She didn't want to anyhow. Their words had been blurring in and out and she didn't know what they were saying. She was now in a room with tubes and wires and beeping, but she could not understand how she got there. It seemed to defy all explanation.

Suckers and Cynics

I've known Jericho Ebb since we were babies in the church nursery together. Our friendship solidified around the age of five when a girl named little Gracie Matthews told everyone that I was a bastard since I didn't have a daddy no more. Jericho fixed that by telling everyone that she was, in fact a dog-faced ass-whore, thereby introducing our entire kindergarten class to the term "dog-faced ass-whore." From then on, we were inseparable.

In the summer of seven years old, Jericho and I hustled kids on a sidewalk in the storefront section of the town of Bethany with a supposed magic trick. Jericho had one of those boxes that could make quarters disappear. The real trick was that he could never get them to reappear. It was our favorite scam back then.

I guess I was what you would call the sensitive one. I spent my time writing bad poetry and trying to read books that were usually above my reading ability. I absolutely loved books. Sometimes, I would make Jericho go down to the bookstore with me to try to buy them, thinking that Jericho would be as enthused as I was, but it never worked out that way. Even at that age, Jericho would just troll for girls and look around in vain for something worth stealing.

One Saturday in particular, I remember my mouth curling up in the anticipation of a book. I had seen the book in the bargain clearance section of the store a few days earlier. It had a wonderful cover with a colorful picture of an evil king and I wanted it more than anything in that moment. I needed it. The book that I just had to have was *The Emperors Clothes*. Okay, it wasn't some great scholarly dissertation, but what would you expect? I was only seven.

I could not uncurl my mouth as Jericho and I walked into that dusty, familiar bookstore and slapped a dollar down on a desk that was being used as a sales counter. My mother had given me that dollar to put in the offering plate at church. I had pocketed the dollar for an occasion like this. The fact that life is unfair is an instinctual knowledge for the have-nots and I knew this early in my childhood. My mother had discovered she had cancer that year and would continually struggle with bouts of malignancy and remission for the next eleven years, but her faith never wavered. As for me, I figured that if life ever became fair, I'd just pay the church with a lump sum donation. The way I figured it, a fair system would be worth the lump sum and more.

After tiring from that and our hustles in the storefront section of town, our next favorite hangout was a fort we had thrown together with old pallets down the road. While heading there, all I was thinking about was my next poem. The book was a nice distraction for a few hours but in that moment, I was beginning to think that maybe I was in love. There was a girl I had seen in town for the first time just before school had let out at the start of June. I didn't know her, but when she looked at me, it felt like the blood went out of my heart. It hurt like going into an overly heated house after being barefoot in the snow. The girl that I was so enamored with was the start of, and would always be, the worst alliteration of my life.

While walking on the sidewalk leading to our tree fort, an older lady with wild eyes was talking out loud to no one and throwing corn at chickens with a particular calm, hate, evilness. Her clothes were tattered and she had hair that looked more like bed head than the intentional wildness of an older lady's hair. Jericho and I spotted her first and, sensing that she was a little crazy, we tried to pass by her without exchanging a greeting or even being noticed.

"What book you got there?" asked the witch of a lady with a voice that sounded like a bag of wet nails. We were wholly petrified as though we were seeing a wrinkled version of the devil incarnate. Then Jericho found his legs and ran away.

"You're a witch, aren't you?" I asked, alone and surprised of my own voice.

"No, but I'll eat your fucking heart if you cross me," snapped the lady. "What book you got there?" She reached out her long, knobby fingers and grabbed my book.

"Oh, *The Emperor's Clothes*. Let me tell you something about *The Emperors Clothes*. It's bullshit and the argument is invalid." The old lady handed the book back to me with a look as if I just insulted her.

"Yes ma'am," I said back. I was trying to listen out of manners, but even at that age I could tell the old lady was as insane as the sky was blue.

"After that king was deemed incompetent and left the town, no one wanted to be the next person to be fooled, so no one in that fucking kingdom saw puppies and elephants in clouds, or listened to music, or hung paintings, or any of that kind of shit. What kind of hell hole does that sound like to you?" she screeched as she violently tossed corn to her chickens.

When the lady eased her wild eyes off me and looked down at the chickens, I saw my chance and ran away to catch up with Jericho, leaving her there to continue talking to herself.

"Fucking kids, thinking I'm a witch. I'll shove a broomstick up their asses," she snarled out loud to herself and the chickens when she noticed that I had run away.

Just before the sun went down on that afternoon, Jericho and I found safety and refuge inside our broken pallet wood fort. Jericho thumbed through the pictures in the brand new book while I was enthralled in drawing a picture out of what felt like necessity to me. In the innocence of my inspiration then, I think I was what all poets are, mediocre and great, before someone tells them different. To me, it felt like I was creating one of the great masterpieces of the world. I could not have been more genuinely inspired while scribbling with that worn nub of a blue crayon.

"It's finally finished!" I exclaimed, squiggling the last line on a piece of construction paper.

Jericho looked up from the book in disgust. "I can't believe you're going to be eight next year and you're still drawing, Johnny. That's so faggoty."

"What do you mean, Jerry?" I asked in a state of confusion and hurt.

"My dad told me that drawing is only for little kids that don't know any better and queer bait that do. I can't believe you didn't know that. I've known that since I was five."

After a long, silent moment of trying to understand, I guess I finally absorbed what Jericho was saying and, for the sake of stupid reasons, resolved to agree. I promptly balled up the drawing and threw it in an unused corner of our fort.

At that moment, all of the mothers of the town of Bethany began calling their kids home for dinner. I left out of the fort and headed home for beans and hoecake, or whatever it was mom had been cooking that night. Jericho stayed in the fort just a little longer. Ten steps out of the fort, I started looking back as I walked home. In hindsight, I think I wanted to believe that Jericho might have gone over to my crumpled blue, waxy drawing and opened it with some kind of inspiration or secret respect. That probably wasn't the case, but it was a nice thought.

The drawing was of a girl. In eight years from that time she would become The Girl. I would often be fooled in love and friendship and human suffering in general. But in the adult years of my life, I would try to remember those times with a glossy haze as the brightest spots in my childhood.

The Encounter

"What the hell are you doing? Come on Al. We've got to get back before dark. I've got a good mind to leave your ass out here," yelled Kohoki. "I'm not going home empty handed. Just go on without me and I'll catch up in a little while," replied Al.

Kohoki and Al lived in a considerably small tribe in an area they called The Safe Territory. This territory was heavily wooded and plush with deer, bear, and all types of greenery. They were both at the age of knowing everything better than the elders and were looking to prove the things they thought they knew by bringing in the largest food bounty the tribe had ever seen. So far they were empty handed.

Al was not willing to accept defeat on the outing. When Al and Kohoki went out on this food quest, they strayed just outside the comfort of The Safe Territory. No one else in their tribe would have approved of this, but what did they know anyway? After hours of nothing, Kohoki was completely over it. "Fine. That's just fine. Keep your ass out here. I'm heading back," she proclaimed, tired, angry and frustrated.

Al walked through the woods in the opposite direction of her, just to spite her. In his anger, he walked for five minutes, then ten minutes, then thirty minutes.

He had gone way off the familiar part of what they knew just beyond The Safe Territory before he realized it. *Where the hell am I going?* he asked himself internally. He began to break a few twigs and shrubbery pieces to ensure that he wouldn't walk in circles as he navigated his way back.

In between snapping twigs, he heard the sound of something moving through the woods. It sounded too big to be a deer and too clumsy to be a bear. The sound was coming from a valley in the forest floor just to his right. Al crouched down, anxiously hoping to spot the creature making the noise. The hair stood up on his arms in the anticipation of a possible bounty.

The creature just looked like a dark blur at first moving through the forest. It was majestic but something was off. And, as the creature walked out into an open spot between two giant trees, Al saw it. It was like nothing he had ever seen. He had heard stories of things like this, but thought that it was just something to scare the children into being good.

What Al had spotted there on the valley of the forest floor was a creature walking on two legs. It definitely was not a bear, but so help him, it was on two legs. The fur of the creature was not like anything he had ever seen. It looked matted, or braided down. It looked like it was matted down into a pattern or something. The creature carried a stick. It was uncanny how similar the creature's movements were to Al's.

Al's blood raced through his veins as he crouched down, trying to be as still as possible. He listened to birds and squirrels of the forest chime loudly. They seemed to be trying to warn the rest of the forest to run. At this point, he wished his anger had not made him deaf to those warnings earlier. He wished he had gone back with Kohoki. He thought the creature might kill him and he told himself that if he somehow got back, he would never argue with her again.

The creature spun around as if it were lost. At first, it began to walk the opposite direction of Al, but then it turned and began walking directly towards him. Al froze. There was nowhere to go. If he ran, the creature would have surely run him down and killed him.

The sound of feet dragging through the leaves got closer and closer. Fear was overtaking Al now. But he had to think. How could he get out of this one? Al closed his eyes and put his head down. When he opened his eyes, he saw a rock.

Of course! he thought. Al picked up the rock and threw it to the left of the creature. He thought that if he could create a sound in another direction, the creature might veer that way instead. Unfortunately for him, the rock hit a tree and ricocheted directly in front of the creature. This made the creature even more curious.

The creature let out a noise. It wasn't really a grunt, but it wasn't really a howl either. It was sort of a mix between the two. This noise sent shivers down Al's spine. Al was out of options. He began to panic.

In his panic, anger began to come over him. If this creature was going to kill him, he was going to have to struggle to do it. Maybe he would even make the creature regret trying in the first place. If this matted haired asshole wanted to kill him, it was going to be a struggle.

Al's anger came to a boil. All of a sudden, he stood up and yelled at the creature. "All right, dickhead. You want to kill me? Come and get me." That split second seemed to last forever as he realized the weight of what he had just done. Fear and common sense got the better of him and he bolted in the opposite direction as fast as he could. After ten minutes, he realized the creature was not running after him. He ran for another fifteen minutes just to be safe.

When Al arrived back to The Safe Territory, his story about the creature with matted fur walking on two legs amazed his tribe. While no one of adult age believed the story, it would be passed down for generations as another cautionary tale of what could happen outside The Safe Territory.

Al's story was real, however. The creature that Al had seen in that part of the woods would go back to its own tribe and tell the story of the creature it had once seen. The name of the creature that Al had seen was Jimmy. Jimmy would run out of the woods and back to his truck that he had parked along the highway. Jimmy would tell his story first at a diner about ten miles from where he had parked his truck to walk into the woods. No one would believe Jimmy either.

The Repetition Mirror (Part I)

The night of a waxing moon drew fog around Davy Burton's rundown camper. The camper looked out of focus through the fog. It appeared as though it should be white, yet it was caked with dirt containing streaks along it as if the last rain storm had cut through the thick layer. Moving to the inside, there was a small open room with wet clay and sculpting tools. Scattered along the floor, there were clutters of art magazines and brushes with dried paint on them. In a raised bed section of the camper laid the contorted figure of Davy Burton, sleeping. He was sweating through blackheads and other puss-filled bumps and snoring uneasily. Suddenly, he sat up in the bed. He walked to the little bathroom, splashed water on his face and his stringy haired, balding head and stared at himself in the mirror. "Holy Shit!" he said.

Abruptly, he bolted out of the bathroom, grabbed huge chunks of clay and began sculpting violently. His facial expressions were that of an obsessed man. As he added clay, he began breathing heavy as though he were running. When he finished, he dropped his mud covered sculpting knife into a water bucket and stood back. He paused for a moment and looked around his sculpture from all angles. He then laughed to himself.

"I thought I had something for a moment there. One day I'll get it," he conceded aloud through his rotted teeth as though he were trying to convince himself.

The next day came hard and fast in the camper. The sun was coming through the windows so thick that it seemed like solid lines. Davy had passed out on the floor right in front of his sculpture. As he started to get up, he looked up at his work.

"What the hell are you looking at? Fuck me. That's a hangover," he yelled toward the modeled clay and put his hand to his head.

He looked down at the floor and then up at the sculpture again and said, "Damn, I thought I had something." Davy set the sculpture on his bed and then walked out of the camper for the start of his day.

Several hours in the day had come and passed in the hole of a camper. Suddenly, there was a knock and the front door opened almost simultaneously. It was Ms. Stewart. She was a nosy cat lady that had taken an interest in Davy a while back. She fantasized about situations in which Davy would be the equivalent of being another one of her pets. He only allowed this fantasy to go on because of the sex. However, this fantasy gave her the determination that a basic door lock without a deadbolt could not stop.

"Daaavvvyyy? Davy? Are you here?" she asked as she continually crept through his living room, which also doubled as his bedroom. Without hesitation, she kept snooping through the camper.

"I just wanted to know if you could come over tonight. I'm making hash in the slow cooker! Are you here?" she asked again.

Abruptly she set her eyes on the sculpture. It hit her dead on. There were no more words. She was having a tortured moment of unrecognizable facial expression. This lasted over a minute. Then her face gradually changed into a look of horror and then a deep sadness. A tear rolled from her eye. She shriveled up into a ball as if she could not take it any longer.

Down the road, Davy Burton was out looking to score breakfast and a bottle of whiskey. He had settled for coffee and a cathead at the local diner. But as he was leaving the diner to head back to his camper, he noticed a horde of people up ahead on the broken concrete sidewalk. There appeared to be a commotion coming from the funeral parlor up on the left. A genuine commotion was a big deal to that small town, so the crowd was pretty large.

"What's going on?" Davy asked a young boy riding his bike around the outside of the congregation.

"It's that old Ms. Stewart lady. She killed herself," the kid said as he rode in circles on the street.

Davy was in shock as he ran over to investigate. The first person he saw was a man named Thad. Before addiction got the better of him, Thad used to play cards with Davy over at the billiard place a few blocks down the road. He wore a patch over his right eye because of a mishap while cooking meth, but would tell everyone it was a lawnmower accident. He always looked to be tweaking. Davy went over to him to ask him about the situation.

"Hey Ol' Thaddeus One-Eye! What's going on here?" asked Davy.

"The weird cat lady said she couldn't live with herself after seeing what she had seen. Apparently, she goes in to Isaac's place and asks to see the coffins. Then, when they walk back to the showroom, she climbs in one with a note and then shoots herself. From what I heard, Isaac grabbed the gun and she only shot off of her lower jaw. They don't expect her to make it, though," Thad reported as they both looked at the scene made by the ambulance and police cars.

"Lydia Stewart? She was fine the other day when she wanted me to, uh, check her plumbing over at her house," said Davy. "What in the hell could have happened since then?"

"I don't know Dave. I guess we'll never know. Hey, if you ever need anything stronger than nose paint, give me a call."

Davy Burton slinked away from the crowd and headed back to his trailer, bemused by the day's events.

That night, the fog crept in again around the late Ms. Stewart's place. She had lived in a small, two bedroom tract home with plastic border fencing around it and blue, plastic shudders on the windows. The county had not yet removed the cats from the property, so there were constant high pitched wails coming from it. The smell of cat litter and piss was unbearable.

Inside the place was surprisingly clean except for the cats and cross stitching supplies covering the living room couches. Down the hall of the house hung pictures of family members that Ms. Stewart had never spoken to and had only seen as a child. In a room at the end of the hall sat a desk. The desk was covered in papers with partial stories written on them. On top of these partial stories was a rough draft of the suicide note she had written that morning after leaving Davy's place.

The note read, "To whomever it may concern, I can no longer live with myself after seeing what I've seen. That sculpture. A simple piece, I would never have thought an intangible object could do that, but with one image, one moment of seeing it, seeing it again, that damn thing ripped my life apart. All of my family, everything I care for. I guess it's all bullshit now. I don't blame Davy for it, but it's too late to take it back now. I bid you all a farewell and fuck off..., P.S. It makes no sense and therefore, it follows that no one should look at that sculpture unless you want your every inclination to be fucking destroyed!"

On the other side of the house, the closet door of the other bedroom was left opened. At the foot of the closet was a clay sculpture done by Ms. Stewart sixteen years prior. There was a macabre presence radiating out of her sculpture, like that of a haunted house or an elderly animal caged in a zoo.

It had been a remarkable piece for a twenty year old, but unremarkable for the world. The sculpture was identical in every way to the sculpture Davy Burton created. In her crazed state, it was never made clear why she didn't just destroy her work or Davy's, given her enmity towards them.

While the news of her death caused a huge stir, Davy was the only person to attend her funeral. No one saw her sculpture or ever fully understood what it was about Davy's piece that caused her to commit suicide, but the news of his sculpture allowed him to sell it for what amounted to a year's worth of his drug of choice, outdated sopers. Some rich man that no one in town knew had bought the work and, other than a newspaper picture, no one in the county ever saw it again. This piece would be the only work of art that Davy would sell in his life.

The Repetition Mirror (Part II)

"You got anything other than that dirt weed?" asked David Burton to a man he had just met standing outside Hillel's Big Gas Convenience Store at 11:45 at night. "I got something from over in Ferllington last week that had me solid for days." Davy Burton was a chronic lost cause. He was a case of disappointment. And now, at the age of forty-five, prospects weren't looking good for him.

His most respectable habit in his spare time, up until a few years prior, was his ambition as a sculptor. He would use all forms of clay and had even worked out a deal with the art teacher in Horwitson to where he would sneak in and use the kiln from time to time. All of this changed when a woman named Lydia Stewart took her own life and mentioned one of his sculptures in her suicide note.

"Naw man. You're coming off too strong. I don't mess with people that haven't been vouched for," said the uncomfortable drug dealer that Davy was being overly enthusiastic towards. The man was wearing a large puffy coat and leaning against the wall of a convenience store. He was trying to act nonchalant, but with his location and attire, he may as well have been walking down the street naked.

"Wait a minute. Don't I know you?" the man asked Davy. "Yeah! I've seen pictures of you. Don't tell me. Oohhh. I know. You're that guy that made that sculpture that was so bad it killed that lady a few years ago!"

"Uh. No. That wasn't me and how do you remember shit like that from so long ago?" Davy asked, less than enthused now.

"Well, for one thing, I dabble in the arts too. I'm just doing this till I get the money together to drop my album. I'm a rapper and my shit is on point. For another thing, I was working at the café right next door when that whole thing went down."

"Well it didn't go down like that," snapped Davy just before sucking his rotted teeth. "I had known Lydia for a long time before then and she was just as crazy before seeing that sculpture as she was after." Davy broke from his perturbed state and smiled. "But if it helps me get some of that stuff in your coat, I'll tell you whatever story you want to hear about that."

The man never did give Davy what he wanted and Davy eventually grew tired of harassing him and started his walk back to his trailer for a beer. While walking back, a stray cat began to follow him. It was an ugly little thing with just one snaggletooth sticking out of the front left side of its mouth. It had a few chunks of fur missing in spots and its left ear was swollen. The cat reminded Davy of Lydia and he felt sorry for it. He let the creature follow him all the way back to his trailer.

When he got back to the trailer, the cat stayed outside the place and meowed in the dark for a little while. Davy decided that he would put out some milk in a bowl for his new found friend, but he soon discovered that all he had in his fridge was half and half, so he poured some of that in a bowl and cut it down a little with some water. The cat seemed more than happy with that when he put it down, but when Davy turned his head away for a moment and then looked back, the bowl was half empty and the cat was gone into the night air.

When he noticed that the cat had disappeared, he thought of Lydia again. Lydia was stuck in his head and to him, she seemed to ruin even the smallest moments like the one he had with the cat. He knew what he had to do to fix things.

On the day after Lydia had committed suicide, Davy snuck back into her house and stole a few things that might allow the police to construe things the wrong way. Mostly he had broken in to her place to take gifts he had given her and some sex toys, but when he saw the exact replica of the sculpture he had created sitting in her closet, he snatched that as well. He didn't know why, but he also took one of Lydia's private journals off her desk.

He had never cracked that journal but on that night, he felt like that would be the only way to purge her memory from haunting him. Before opening the journal, he took out her sculpture that he had stolen and placed it on his coffee table. He thought about how amazing it was that he would have created almost an exact replica of it years later without ever having seen hers.

As he pulled out her journal, he grabbed a beer and plopped down on his faded, brownish-yellow, plaid couch and propped his worn, holey boots up on top of the sculpture. The sculpture looked to be a cubist piece that contained elements of the bust of a man. Davy took a long sip from the neck of his beer bottle and opened the journal.

Two and a half hours later, Davy's eyes were wide and his mouth was open as he slammed the pages shut. He had learned Lydia was admitted to the Kippalville State Lunatic Asylum back in 1967 at the age of eighteen. The place would close down in 1973, but the things that had gone on in that asylum were notorious. Her journal talked of some of those things. It talked of the people and the food, but mostly, it talked of Dr. Malico.

Dr. Malico was the psychiatric doctor of her ward and she had an enormous crush on him. It wasn't very long before he noticed this. Most doctors may have quashed this puppy love or at least ignored it. Dr. Malico however, went another way.

When Lydia was twenty years old, she worked to express herself in the asylum through an art program. She would sculpt pinch pots and coffee mugs, but she loved the free expression and abstraction of Cubist sculpture.

Being avant-garde was all the rage in higher society at the time and, while she was a little behind the times, she wanted to try her hand in it. She did a bust of Dr. Malico, only she decided to add some elements of her newly found Cubist style.

On her birthday, she showed him her proud masterpiece, alone in her room. Her heart was racing. A few moments later on that day, she learned in the worst of ways that Malico was not a good doctor or even a good person. In the dark of her room, her face was shoved into her bed by the doctor as he proceeded to rape her. From the angle of her head being shoved into the mattress, the only thing she could see during the traumatic event was that damned sculpture that had seemed so beautiful only a few moments earlier. She never told anyone about the rape and she carried her sculpture with her throughout her life as though it were her burden to bear.

The realization of the psychology behind Lydia taking her life had not hit Davy until that moment. The time was now 3:00 am and Davy decided right then and there that he was going to go visit the long since abandoned mental hospital in Kippalville. He took a deep breath and started out of the door without packing. He had enough money for the bus ticket considering that the convenience store gentleman didn't sell him anything and he figured he could sleep on the bus.

As he walked out the door, he looked over his shoulder at the sculpture on his coffee table. "Dammit,

Lydia. I guess, here we go again," he mumbled as he slammed his trailer door for the last time. In a sense, Lydia had bequeathed this burden to Davy. There would be no ultimate outcome in Kippalville for Davy, though. David Burton was murdered on the way to the bus station by a gentleman in a puffy jacket trying to rob him. In his last moments on a sidewalk with a lacerated kidney, he would chuckle at the irony that the only thing Lydia Stewart had left behind after death was the part of her past that she had spent the rest of her life wanting, but not allowing herself to get beyond.

A Life in Landscaping

"That lady was primed and ready to switch to Dalton Brothers Life. Why do you keep fucking with my livelihood, Georgie?" said Adam.

"You know, us simple minded minions of the world gots to do whats we cans to ekes out a livin' in this day and age. Not all of us can be the great Adam McDonald, King of life insurance," George retorted sarcastically.

Prior to their truck ride, George Thatcher had spotted Adam McDonald on The Widow Welch's porch with his best life insurance pitch. George promptly walked over to them and explained to the Widow that the fine print of the paperwork showed that she would be paying $70 a month. Once she realized the true cost, she politely declined and closed her door on Adam.

"You know I'd give you a job if that's your issue," said Adam.

"Shit, you know I can't be a nine to fiver," mumbled George while looking down at the floorboard.

"I know. It's just that this landscaping thing you do... I mean, don't get me wrong, I like to have a nicely mowed lawn as much as anybody, but...I mean it's a nice hobby, but it's not a living," said Adam.

"It's just this weird feeling I have. Like this is what I am meant to do. It makes me happy," said George.

"Well, if you're going to do it, do it. Get past it. Then come work for me," said Adam.

The truck pulled up a hill and into the yard of a two-story southern estate. The overall look of the place was that of a plastic wasteland. There were pink flamingos in the yard, giant walls of vinyl siding, and artificial grass rugs on the porch. Matilda McDonald walked out on the porch to greet the two. She was a beautiful woman with a southern drawl and seemed to be the only thing that wasn't kitschy in the whole yard. George and Matilda had shared a kiss in high school and had always felt weird about it to the point that neither of them had ever told Adam.

"Georgie Thatcher!" said Matilda as she ran out and hugged him. As Matilda hugged him, George slightly hesitated before reciprocating.

"Well I haven't seen you since that little incident when you attended our church!" exclaimed Matilda.

"Yeah, uh, I'm awful sorry about that. I wished I'd a known that those hymnals were under the pews and I wouldn't a made my own words to those songs," explained George.

About a month prior, there was an incident where a hung over George Thatcher stood clumsily amidst a row of pews in church. He was singing lyrics about crying in his beer to the tune of a gospel song about how God lifts people up. This really tested the Christian inclinations of their congregation.

"Well never-the-less, you're still invited here. You have to have supper with us and I won't take no for an answer," replied Matilda.

"Well, when a pretty lady asks me for supper, the only answer I can give her is yes," said George.

The look of the inside of the southern estate was how anyone may have pictured it. George, Adam, and Matilda had just finished supper and were sitting with plates at a breakfast nook from which the kitchen could be seen. The cabinets were typical chicken wire, and the overall feeling of the place was that it must have been inherited from a long dead relative and never updated.

"So Georgie, Adam says you're going to work with him from now on. That seems pretty exciting!" said Matilda as she squeezed Adams's hand.

George took a sip of his can of beer and paused after setting it down. "I've got some other things to finish before I can get to that point, Matty," said George.

"He wants to cut a few more lawns before he'll join us. Perhaps he could cut our grass here, Matty," Adam said.

George dropped his head as though he were embarrassed at first then looked up and into Matilda's eyes. There was a moment of silence. Then George raised his beer before speaking. "I think Matilda is doing a great job on the lawn around here without my help."

"Well you better find a shit ton more lawns to cut if you don't want to starve. Matty, what do you think about all of his 'Oooohhh, I wanna cut grass' crap?" asked Adam.

"Well I think it's noble," said Matilda.

"OK. Well here's to the two best looking people in town and this noble asshole, pardon my French," said Adam as he toasted his glass.

As the night began drawing to an end, Adam walked outside and sat on the porch of his southern estate smoking a cigar and reflecting on the past. The thing about Adam was that he had fought in Vietnam and often stared deeply into nothing. He would always tell Matilda that he couldn't remember anything much about it when she would ask. The only solid fact she and George knew was that he had seen combat over there. The truth was that, while he loved to talk, he kept that part of him separate from the ones he loved. On a tip from an army buddy, he had come back home and put all his money into an upstart life insurance business.

George opened the door to join Adam. There was a moment of silence. "You know, I'm expanding operations all the way to Brannen," said Adam, cutting through the thick silence.

"I wanted to thank you for dinner. Matty is such a delight. You know, you did the best you could possibly do when you married that woman," said George.

"Don't hit me with all that proper thanking and shit. You're still a fucking ass-douche. You sit there in some broken down shack on the outside of town like some smack junky and talk about some magic moment when you get your shit together. And me, like an asshole, I can't help but always be here for you. It just makes me want to shit on your pillow," said Adam.

"Well, from the bottom of my heart, and from one asshole to another, go fuck yourself, uh, I mean thank you. I know what I'm giving up. I can't help but see it every time I see you and Matty together," said George. Then George started off the porch to head back to his bed.

George would continue landscaping for fifteen more years before passing away. He had a beautiful, quiet funeral that Adam had paid for. In the fifty three years that Adam and Matilda were married, Matilda never told Adam about the silly little high school kiss between her and George.

Stagnation of Regrets

Joanna Howell walked through the woods for what felt like forever for her. She had grown up out in those woods and so she was never lost. She had always known where to make a turn or veer around a stump. A long time ago, she and Katie Simms had set up a sparse series of rope pieces placed high up in the trees so as no one else would notice them. The rope pieces had dry-rotted on those high branches, but they were still there.

Joanna had come back home for good after a seven year hiatus and was heading out to the woods to take her turn for the night shift at the moonshine still. As she got closer to the still, the woods opened up as if it appeared out of nowhere.

There was only a small patch of high ground in the swamp where someone could build a still and both she and Katie did. They had spent two weeks looking for that perfect spot years ago when they were looking to build it. Many times, they had thought they had found the best place, but Katie always rejected it. She'd say, "We're not only looking for just the wise and practical spot. We're looking for the right spot. This is our little secret in the world where, if we're having a bad day or something, we can think about it and smile. We know what that is, we just have to find it." That search was the most poetic Joanna had ever seen Katie.

When they had found this spot, Joanna had assumed Katie would turn it down like every other spot, but Katie accepted it whole heartedly. Katie asked her if she had felt like it was right and Joanna would have said yes to anywhere at that point. She was relieved when the hunt was over.

That same relief came back to Joanna then as she was walking up to the still. Katie was sitting there in a lawn chair when Joanna arrived. Katie had been maintaining their still and their side business during those past seven years and was secretly elated to have help for a change even though she didn't want to show it. Inside the shed, the still itself looked as if it had just finished a batch and then been wiped down.

"It looks like you've been coming out here a lot, lushy," Joanna jested. Katie just nodded her head in a serious tone. Spending the noon hours of the day in the middle of a swamp talking to herself had brought back tougher memories.

"Yeah, I still come out here every two days. Now that you're back, maybe it will be like the good ol' days," said Katie.

"You didn't leave anything in the still. You never did believe in sour mash," Joanna said in an effort of small talk.

"Sour mash is just a cheap way to complicate an easy process. Sometimes you have to pay extra for quality," Katie replied, breaking away from her sadness.

"Hey, do you remember when we pissed off those college kids by selling them the water from the worm box? It took half an hour, but you convinced them it was actually better. You called it 'The Grappa of the Moonshine World,' we got the hell out of Dodge before that played out," Joanna laughed.

"You're going to need a bed," Katie said.

"I'll be fine without one. Truth is I never do sleep that well in them. All they do is hurt my back."

"I got you this police scanner. I'll bring you some crossword puzzles tomorrow," said Katie. "Do you have anything to eat? What about water?" she went on before Joanna interrupted.

"Will you just go on? I'll be here in this same spot tomorrow. You can check on me then," Joanna urged.

Katie finally left and Joanna sat in a lawn chair in the loud silence of the woods with only her thoughts for company. Shadows crawled across the floor for entertainment. Sitting there, she imagined what life would have been like if she hadn't left town with Kevin Downey when she was nineteen. Katie kept materializing her mind.

She flipped on the police scanner as a distraction. A song from when she was younger ran through her head.

It was about letting go of a beautiful girl for the sake of saving her. She hummed the tune out loud and then whistled for a moment, but the song was a little too closed to home, so she closed her eyes and waited for the morning when Katie would be back for her shift out by their still. The two women would never discuss why Joanna left in the first place with Kevin those years ago. They would always be moderately successful with their business and moderately sad with their friendship.

A Translation of Small Talk

A young man sat silently in a doctor's office waiting room listening to the clicking of the clock on the wall. He had been the only person in the waiting room for the past ten minutes, save for the receptionist, when an older man came in. After a brief and awkward sign-in, the old man sat down in the chair opposite of the young man so that they were facing each other. The young man looked up in a quick moment and accidentally caught the eye of the older man.

"How you doing," the old man asked a young man. Loosely translated, this meant, "Now that we've made eye contact, I feel obligated to give you some kind of greeting. I'm going with a basic question because somewhere down the line, someone thought this question was the least aggressive greeting and now, it's been said so many times that it just comes out without any thought. Please just respond with 'fine, thanks' and we can go back to looking in other directions."

"Could be worse. How about you?" said the young man. Loosely translated this meant, "Even though your greeting was an obligation of basic courtesy, I'm bored. We are going to sit here uncomfortably for at least the next five to ten minutes and so I am going to either make you respond back with something or have us sit here in the even more awkward silence of an unanswered question.

"Not too bad," said the old man. "If it gets any hotter outside the soles of our shoe are going to melt." This unassuming statement was a bold move by the old man. The basic translation of this was, "Okay. If we are going to play that game, it's time to go big or go home. I see your talk about personal wellness and I'll raise you absent minded talk about the weather. Now you'll have to not respond and seem impersonal, agree with my trivial assumption, or disagree with it like a lunatic.

The young man had a big choice to make. He wanted to pretend that he had a message on his cell, but he had left his phone in his car. He wondered for a moment if he could mime the action of a phone convincingly, but he ultimately decided to respond to the old man's statement. "Yep," he said. "It's this humid heat, too. Some rain would cool us off for a little while, anyway. It's a shame. All this humidity and no rain." This was a brilliant move by the young man. Instead of a basic defensive tactic like "Yes sir, and it's only going to get hotter," he went on the offensive by adding rain into the conversation. It was the basic equivalent of saying, "I can do this all day. How far do you want to take this, old man?"

"My garden could sure use some rain. The only things that seem to not mind the heat are the weeds," said the old man as he smiled. They were whole heartedly stuck in the mindless conversation now and both of them knew it. Loosely translated, the old man's words meant, "I grew up in a time when this was the only conversation we had. Even with loved ones. I've had way more practice at this and I can go all day. Keep it up and I'll take this all the way to the color of our socks and what my kidney stone felt like."

For a moment, the young man thought about steering the conversation away from the weather and move right into a picture of his little girl. He thought that might make the old man regret his decision to talk. A second thought flashed through his head of having to look at a thousand pictures of the old man's grandkids and he decided not to go that route. "Weeds would be just about the only thing I could grow," retorted the young man. This was a safer play than the pictures strategy. This translated into, "Look, neither one of us wants this. Let's just cut our losses and end it right here."

"I think I have a picture of my garden from just before the drought," said the old man. This was a cruel and vicious move. It roughly translated into, "Hell no. You've made me come this far and we are finishing this." The young man wondered why on earth anyone would carry a picture of their garden with them. He figured the old man must get into many of these situations and this must be one of his common strategies.

"Reallly?" The young man said with a smile. He looked over at the picture in the old man's hand and nodded. "That's beautiful. I bet in person, that thing is really magnificent." This towed the line of being a little too personal. He had just met the old man and he was talking about seeing his garden in person. The young man knew that this would be a big risk, but he was ready to end the conversation and he was almost ready to go full on polite creepy to do it. The young man gave a quick glance at the door where the physician's assistant would call them back for their appointments, but there was no assistance to be had.

"Well I just live two blocks from here. Maybe you could come over sometime and see the garden," said the old man. As the words were coming out of his mouth, the old man knew he had overplayed his hand. Although it wasn't what he meant, this loosely translates to, "This really is fun! We should do this again as soon as possible!" His left eye twitched at the realization of this. Sometimes no one wins.

Suddenly in a perfectly timed stroke of luck, the physician's assistant called the young man's name. "Thank God," he thought to himself. That was a close call. As he stood, the physician's assistant called the old man's name as well. "Quit following me," the young man joked as the physician's assistant walked them back to their respective examining rooms.

"See you on the other side," said the old man. At that point, the two men thought the conversation was over. It was a close call, but the old man had won the battle. "Say," said the young man, not ready to be defeated. "You wanna grab some lunch after this?"

"That sounds wonderful!" said the old man, knowing full-well that he couldn't say no without conceding. After the appointment, all that either man wanted to do was go home, but because neither conceded, they both left out of the doctor's office for lunch together, both dying a little on the inside.

Happenstance at a Bar

That Wednesday evening was particularly cold for the city of Clamport. A few snow flurries had blown across the lake earlier that day and most of the people of that area had begun preparing for the larger storm projected to hit them that night. The glow of the streetlights had barely cut through the night air and the first snow of that season.

Carl Roberts threw back a shot of vodka in a small hotel bar called Liquor McVicker's. He was not from that area and he knew no one in the locale. He had gone downstairs to that bar to help him escape that lonely fact. The bar was busy, but not crowded when he signaled to the bartender that he would like another shot.

After downing his second shot, he starred at his shot glass and noticed a small piece of food stuck on the side. As he scratched at it, he couldn't decide if it was from salad dressing or gravy from a previous patron and, while he was a little off-put, it did not stop him from asking for an old-fashioned and picking up a menu.

"What's your story?" asked the gentleman three stools down from him at the bar as he stared at his menu. The man had a slightly slurred speech and he appeared to be around four to five beers or two to three drinks in.

"I'm not from here. Just passin' through. I'm from up near Mullverston," Carl replied without even looking over at the man.

"I'm not from here either. I just thought we could stare at those women over there and tell stories and bullshit for a while," said the man that had closed the gap on the barstool space and was sitting next to Carl. "I'm Barton Fosse from over in Sanjack and I'm stuck here in this god forsaken place for at least two more days until my rig is fixed."

Barton was a recently divorced trucker. He was slightly balding and self-conscious about it. His divorce had left him both lonely and bitter. He bought a shot for Carl and they spent the next hour getting even more plastered. Carl told the story of how he decided to become a railroad engineer and Barton told the story of how driving long haul was always his destiny. During that time, the crowd thinned out to three tables and the two men at the bar. The lights of the bar flickered twice and the bartender rolled her eyes at their bullshit about three times.

The two men would catch a glimpse of what looked to them to be a group of women in their thirties sitting at one of the tables. The women were getting louder as the night went on. "I bet you don't have enough hair on your ass to go talk to them," dared Barton to Carl.

"Oh, this ought to be good. I've got a shot with your name on it that says you won't do it!" said the bartender, hoping to break the monotony of being the only sober person in a room of drunks.

Carl considered himself to be too old for what he considered to be high school shit, but the bet made him feel younger at the time. After a little more taunting, he stood up to walk over and make his move. Luckily for him, two of the women were walking up to the bar to get more drinks as he stood up.

When he stood up, he turned around and faced directly in front of the two women at the bar. One of the women had blond hair that cut off sharply at her shoulders. She was glowing and seemed really happy. The other woman had brunette hair and carried a permanent scowl. She was definitely older than the happy woman and seemed very irritated with him standing there, preparing to talk to them. He chose the happy faced, blond haired woman. Carl took a deep breath before looking directly in her eyes and speaking.

"What's your name?" He knew he was speaking with slurred speech but, to his way of thinking, he'd rather get rejected for being drunk than get rejected for being a creep. The thought that he could come across as both never entered his mind. The irritated woman immediately jumped in front of the happy lady and prepared to speak. Carl felt the eyes of the other two tables and the bartender on him.

"I don't think she's going to be interested in anything you have to say. She's getting married tomorrow," interrupted the irritated woman.

"Well, what about you?" asked Carl in the most charming voice that a man with six shots and five drinks could summon.

"I'm HER mother!" she exclaimed.

Carl was a little embarrassed, but could not leave it at that. "But I don't see a Mr. HER mother around, so how are you doin' on this lovely evening?" he asked in a last ditch effort. All three tables and the bartender chimed in with low smirking laughter.

He received a pretty good sized welt in the shape of a hand on his face for his efforts, but he drank three more shots that night and did not have to pay for them. Although he never saw Barton again, Barton always kept that as one of his favorite stories to tell at a bar. Carl was so drunk, however, that when he remembered that night, it was Barton and not he that approached the women. When the ladies would tell that story, they always made Carl out to be uglier, drunker, and a lot less intelligent, but the punchline would always get laughs for them as well.

Preying Moon

Dale Mason walked out of the police station weakened and ready to sleep in his own bed. As he waited on the curb for his buddy, Henry Zimmer to swing by and pick him up, he played with his wedding ring and thought about the choices he had made in the week prior. Edna, his wife of almost three years, would have been at the police station, but the couple only had one vehicle between them and he didn't exactly let her know when he was getting out of jail. Besides that, their one and only vehicle was impounded upon Dale's arrest.

Dale was getting out on parole for poaching. A week prior, he had been driving by a field when a couple of deer ran out in front of him and into a field. Without thinking about it, he pulled out his spotlight and shined the field. His intentions were really to spot the trails of the deer as they went in the woods on the far end of the field, but in his daze he had forgotten that he had a loaded shotgun in his gun rack from hunting that morning. This, combined with a handful of priors, left him in a world of uncertainty.

"Get on the ground motherfucker," yelled the ranger that caught him as he buried the barrel of his pistol into the back of Dale's neck. When Dale hit the ground, the barrel of the pistol was traded in for the ranger's knee.

"Please move asshole. I'm just itching to help the grass grow on this road," whispered the ranger in his ear.

A week later, Dale's friend Henry turned into the police station in a rusted out minivan. Henry was a young man from out of Texas that thought being a man meant acting like a cowboy. His minivan had no air conditioner, but it did not matter as his passenger side window had been busted out.

"How's it goin' bud?" asked Henry in an attempt at conversation.

"You see it," replied Dale. Dale was not ready for conversation after spending the last week resting his head on a concrete wall.

As they drove away from the jail, Henry turned abruptly down a road heading away from Dale's house. "Where are you going, dipshit?" Dale asked, thinking Henry just made a wrong turn.

"Cool your burners there, pot rustler. I just have to make a quick stop before dropping you off. It won't take long," Henry replied.

As they began to ease below the pine trees, the two men turned down a stretch of road the locals called Farmer's Row. There were six farms along this stretch of road and not much else. The attraction to this road was that there was a lot of deer and hog traffic that crossed it. Henry eased off the gas and began looking deeply into the fields off the road. Peanuts were the major crop that year and the deer could not stay away.

"Man, I gotta get home to Edna. I ain't got time for this shit right now," intervened Dale as he waved his hands to illustrate his point.

"Just past this field and then I'll turn around," negotiated Henry. Dale did not reply, except for his look of being pissed off.

Once they passed the field, Henry pulled his truck into a turn off that lead into a field in order to turn around and head to Dale's house. Dark was creeping in thick over the green rows of the fields by now. Henry miscalculated where he turned in though, as he spotted the headlights of another vehicle coming down the road. Because of this, he decided to go a little ways further in the turn in to see if there was a place to turn around, rather than just back out onto the road. Thirty feet off the road, he realized that would not be the case. The headlights of the other vehicle lit up the inside of the minivan as it pulled behind them and then those lights began to mingle with blue lights. Panic set in for Henry.

"Shit, shit, shit," Henry repeated.

"Relax. We're not doing anything wrong, peckerwood," Dale said, trying to comfort Henry.

"You don't understand. I have a loaded rifle under the back seat. I have coke in the glove box. And I have an unregistered Colt. We are fucked," Henry said as he opened the door and began to flee into the rows of peanuts.

"I'm not moving. I'm not doing anything wrong. I didn't do anything wrong. I'm not – fuck it!" said Dale as he made a last minute decision to jump out of the van himself and make a run for it. Dale ran in the darkness as he heard voices behind him yell, "Do you see him?" "Not yet, but we'll find him." "There's nowhere to hide."

Dale made it all the way to the closest edge of the field and could just make out a fence post. He tried to leap over where he estimated the two strands of barbed wire that had been put up as a grazing fence were. However, it was so dark that he did not see the pine tree on the other side of the fence and his leap was stopped by the full force of a tree. For a moment, he thought he had been shot or possibly hit by a pair of brass knuckles. His face was now bleeding and scraped up from his face-first jump into the tree and all he could do was stay down and hope he wasn't spotted.

He watched flash lights going around the field and he buried his bloody face in the dirt. All he wanted to do was go home. He felt his heart racing and he thought about Edna. He didn't realize it at the time, but his heavy breathing was giving away his position. He only heard the sound of two steps in the dirt before he felt the familiar press of cold metal into the back of his neck.

"I got you now! I'm gonna blow your damn head off," the voice growled. The voice seemed very familiar to Dale. "Now stand up and dance a jig, motherfucker."

"What?" questioned Dale as he still lay frozen on the ground.

"You heard me, Dale," replied the growling voice. Dale turned to see one of his long time drinking buddies, Arlo Bowen. The reality began setting in that this whole experience was just an elaborate prank.

"You son-of-a-bitch," Dale exclaimed, still unsure about how to feel. He wanted to kiss the air and punch out Arlo at the same time.

Arlo popped the top of a can of beer and handed it to Dale. "You're gonna need this after you change your pants," he said laughing.

It was hard for Dale but after a few days, he would forgive Henry and Arlo for the prank. He would always be on the lookout for their next trick, though. He would also start spending more time with Edna. Their relationship would always be a trying one. They would not always be good for each other, but they would always there for each other. After that week and the bloody-faced finale of it, he would never shine a field for as long as he lived.

A Reluctant Mentor

"Excuse me, Sir. Is there any way you could spare some change?" asked Larry Whyte from the edge of a sidewalk about a block from the grocery store.

At that point, Larry had been homeless for five years. His dissention into homelessness five years prior was less like a spiral and more like a drop. He had originally come to the point of being homeless in the spring when the weather made it not seem so bad. The first winter in the street however, reminded him of why he had put up with so much rush hour traffic and office bullshit in the first place. By the time the third winter had rolled around, Larry was well versed on the ins and outs of being a bum in a small town. He had his own spot on the sidewalk and the police had started leaving him alone.

In another life, Larry was a banker with a bright future. He was on track to fill the position in the Ambling Bank and Trust in the next town over when Big Bob Plimpton was set to retire. When his wife left him, Larry went downhill fast. It wasn't that he got in to drugs or drank heavily. He just really stopped caring. He lost his job and walked away from friends offering to help.

"Hey bud, how's this corner working out for you?" asked a young twenty-something kid with a Vietnam War era jacket. Larry looked up at him squinting as though he were mystified and angry about it.

The young man's name was Noah Belding. He was out there to rebel against his parents, but he was yet to know what that would entail. Being homeless was a romantic notion. He was yet to experience a full winter outside. He was yet to experience fighting with someone over a street corner or waking up to someone pissing on his head. It was all still just an experimental phase with infuriating his parents. Larry had sensed these things about the young man and dreaded the fact that he now had to play a wise sage that hated the life of scratching out a living on the sidewalk.

"I've wasted my life," said Larry, jumping right into the role. "I thought I was being adventurous by dropping acid when I was a sophomore in college. Now look at me. The only woman I ever loved hauls ass the moment things get rough, I can't sit still long enough to keep anything down, and I can't quit shaking. I've been thinking a lot about what living on this street means. I wish it were something profound. It's funny. First the acid, then my sweet Sara, and now I gotta deal with assholes like you coming up to me like it's a goddamn picnic and I'm serving up potato salad. I guess, for some men to love, they have to get bombarded with piles of shit."

Noah's smile ended and he didn't say another word to Larry. "Loony bunch of fucking weirdos around here," he mumbled to himself as he walked away.

Noah would go back to his parents a week later. He saw Larry once more months later and gave him a sawbuck. Larry was presumed to have left town a year later and his whereabouts stayed unknown until 1994 when his body was discovered in a ditch beside the train tracks about a mile outside of the rail yard. The coroner said Larry must've never seen the train coming.

Nights of Eidolon

"You see that tree over there, Bobby? That's how I'm gonna go. I'm getting sick of this place and it won't be long now, and when I've really had enough, I think sixty miles per hour into that tree ought to do it. Don't you think?" Pat said as he and Bobby sat in a parking lot beside the intersection of Abernathy Street and Woodruff Avenue.

They had been drinking a little. They had been smoking a little. They had taken a few pills of which neither could pronounce the names of. Pat's proclamation was not a new revelation for Bobby. Every time they got stoned together, Pat would go off into some long spiel on how driving into that damn tree would be his piece de resistance.

"I know man. You're killing my buzz with that shit. How about this? What if there's a better tree out there just waiting for you to drive into, but you've already committed to that one? I'm just thinking maybe you should keep your options open and shop around. But that's just me," Bobby kidded, hoping Pat would see how silly the tree idea was.

"Nah man. That's the tree. Between the intersection and the line of trees behind it, that's the one," claimed Pat. "It frames it perfectly."

"Ok," said Bobby, "It's a nice frame and all, but you'd be there all broken to hell for what, like an hour or less before the EMTs get you? And that's another thing.

104

You'd be making all those people do so much extra work. If it were me, I'd just go out to the beach and start swimming. No fuss. No muss."

Pat sat quiet for a few minutes. He wanted to retort, but he had no comeback. Then he finally broke his silence. "I see what you're saying. It's just, I don't make dramatic scenes. I never have. The last thing I do on earth though, I want that to be something special. I can't be much, but I can be the story people tell when they get in to work late. I can be the reason some guy twenty five cars back is so angry. I can be the cause of an extra tight hug that a mother gives to her kid when she gets home. And I can be all these things with one simple feat that would just so happen to be my last act on earth."

"Wow man. That seems fucked up. You've never said that before," said Bobby. "You always give some kind of reason, but that is the scariest one I've heard yet."

"What do you mean?" asked Pat.

Bobby closed his bloodshot eyes for a moment before resigning to give the most honest answer he could. "Well I've tried this many times before and it never works, but I'm going to level with you. We have this same talk, with these same beers, with this same herb every single night. Hell, even the smoke wafts in the same pattern. I've tried everything to stop this from happening, but it always does. I've even tried jumping out of the truck and running away. You still decide to ram the truck into that tree and I wind up right back here trying to talk you out of it as though that never happened. If you weren't so damn hard headed. I give up. You do your thing with the depression and all that, but I'm going to at least get high as fuck until we hit the repeat button," he said.

Pat's mouth dropped open and he began with the quiet routine again. After a minute or two, he began to speak. "So I think you are obviously full of shit. You don't like the tree idea, but you're saying my plan is inevitable? You were trying to talk me out of it before, but you pretty much said it's inevitable?"

"Look man, I'm just saying I don't care anymore. Just give me a few more minutes before you crash us into that tree," said Bobby.

"Dude, I think you need to put down that stuff for a while. It might be laced with something else. It's fucking with your head," Pat said.

At that moment, Pat decided against his tree crashing idea. He was never going to go through with it. It was just talk to pass the time. He looked over at the tree a little closer. It was a strong oak tree that must've been over a hundred years old. There was a small pile of trash left at the bottom of the tree. Its branches draped over the top of the street and the stop light wires at the intersection mingled in and disappeared with the tree's foliage and moss.

The bark though. The bark of the tree looked like it was crawling. Was the tree pulsing? It looked like it was pulsing to him. Pat's head got light and it was as if he could hear the tree pulsing. The ground felt like it was leaving him. Then he blanked out. It felt violent just before it went dark, but it was all over.

Pat had gone into a seizure just after putting the truck in gear to go home. In his condition, his foot would mash down all the way on the pedal and he would go over the curbs and ram straight into the tree. The combination of sheared metal, broken glass, and unidentifiable biological parts strewn across the tree and the road was horrendous. The scene would always get misdiagnosed as a murder suicide for Pat and Bobby. Accidents happen and mistakes are always made.

And just as mistakes are always made, the real mistake was not the misdiagnosis of murder at the scene. You see, this was the seventeenth time that Bobby collided with the tree. It was just one out of the one thousand two hundred and forty three times he would experience it. This scene was supposed to be a version of hell. It was supposed to be eons of a person's soul suffering as it struggled to burn off its bad parts that would not let go of the deeds committed to and against it. And it worked like a charm.

The only problem was that it was not supposed to be Bobby's hell. It was not supposed to be Pat's hell and it was not supposed to be the EMTs hell. The hell for which this scene was meant was the pile of trash at the bottom of the tree. That small pile of trash was actually a person. It was actually a drifter. He had been known to have killed four different women in four different cities already and he had just killed his fifth victim that night before going into a drunken stupor and passing out under the oak tree.

Bobby's hell was supposed to last three hundred and forty three times. It was supposed to be a replaying of the time he bullied a kid at school and the way he felt after cheating on his girlfriend. Instead, the killer was spending his hell reliving his fifth victim's murder like a highlight reel while Bobby was reliving their violent deaths over and over. Sometimes life isn't fair, but sometimes death isn't either. Perhaps ghosts are just souls trapped in someone else's hell.

A Conversation on Art

It was mid-afternoon in the town of Happleton. Joe Samson had gone to the high school to try and discuss art with the art teacher, Lou Playnar. The two were not friends and Mr. Playnar appeared to be annoyed by Joe. Joe was in his early twenties and oblivious to the fact that even though Mr. Playnar taught art, he was not passionate about it. The classroom that they were standing in had easels in a circle around a still life that had a football trophy. The art teacher, Mr. Playnar was a round man with an awkward physique, like that of Balzac in a Members Only jacket.

"Did you see that article about the guy that paints things with the things that he wants to paint?" asked Joe. Joe was speaking about an article he had read with pictures that showed a gentleman painting a still life with fish. However, instead of using a paintbrush, the gentleman was using a fish.

"No, I don't believe I did," said Mr. Playnar.

"Well, how about the one where the guy stands in a tree and tries to drip paint on the canvas below in the shape of the wildlife he's watching?" asked Joe, desperate for conversation. In this article, the man was showing how he broke an arm, leg, and pelvis having attempted this and fallen out of the tree.

"You know Joey, I'm not here for art. I don't really give a goddam gobbly gook about some idiot that likes sniffing raw fish or dripping jizz into his mouth and sneezing on a canvas," said Mr. Playnar pointedly. "I put up with a bunch of light loafered kids and young girls with daddy issues for one reason. Football! Next spring I'll be offensive coordinator! We have that Saul Majors kid at quarterback and a great chance at State! After that, who knows? Maybe I'll get a job offer for head coach out in Zanoah. I hear that coach is on his way out."

Joe Samson was momentarily taken back by Mr. Playnar's reply. "Well then, in that case, I wish you a good day sir," said Joe as he put his hat on and tipped it. He turned to walk away, but then stopped and turned back to speak.

"Oh and by the way, that Saul Majors kid is great on his feet, but afraid to get hit. The right side of your offensive line is losing your best tight end, Gabriel Hendrix. With no one to replace him, your boy's going to have to scramble. We all know your wide receiver sucks with audibles. He's great in the middle of the field, but on a scramble you're fucked. The defense is shit and the offense couldn't pour piss out of their cleats if the instructions were written on the fucking soles. Good luck Playnar," said Joe with a brand of poise one only gets by stepping on another man's plan.

As he started to walk away, he looked at a canvas on one of the easels. "That one's pretty good," he touted before walking out the classroom.

Lou Playnar shook his head as though he were getting yelled at by an unruly child and went back to creating football hypotheticals on a piece of paper. He would leave the next year to go to Zanoah and would only come back to Happleton to visit his relatives. He was the special teams coach in Zanoah for thirteen years. He never did accomplish his dream of being the head coach for a high school football team.

The Thing about Three Legged Deer

"Good evening. It is forty three degrees outside.
No chance of rain on the horizon and in local news, it looks
like the Goshen Giants will go on to the Rosemary League
playoffs next Tuesday. In a letter from his publicist, local
writer Orville Baxter, writer of the book *The Gateway to
Hello* will hold a book signing at our own The Dog Eared
Page Bookstore on Saturday. In other news..." roared the
radio. Harvey Taylor turned off the radio after that
announcement. His mind finally let him stop thinking
about the argument that he had gotten into with Jenny
Hastings earlier in the day.

"Of all the lines to draw in the sand, why the hell
did I make it about how many beers to drink during a ball
game?" he thought to himself. Harvey had just broken up
with Jenny two hours earlier. They had been living
together for two months after a year of dates and
weekend sleepovers. That afternoon, they had gotten into
a knockdown, drag out over how towels should be folded.
This of course, stemmed from and became the perfect
platform for Harvey's drinking habit.

In the aftermath of this argument, Harvey
retreated to a small hunting cabin in the woods. This
cabin was his grandfather's and he only used it for an

occasional drinking weekend. He wanted to go back to Jenny almost as immediate as his declaration to her that he was leaving, but that would mean a suffocating bombardment of his ego that he was just not ready to deal with. He had thought about ending things with Jenny a million times before then, but he knew those impulses were mostly alcohol.

He stared in the bathroom mirror and tried to imagine what he had initially thought just before leaving. How was he going to salvage this one? It was no use. All he could think about was getting a beer and his bed.

The sun was going into dusk as Harvey sat on the bed in his cabin lost in thought. Suddenly, there was the sound of something heavy walking in the swamp around the outside of the cabin and then the rustle of leaves and the sound of broken sticks. Half worried it may have been a squatter or a thief, he walked outside the cabin to inspect.

Less than ten yards away, he saw a whitetail deer set against the backdrop of the sun setting through the trees. It seemed so abstract and so real at the same time. Then the deer took a stumbled step out of the line of sight of the sun. It looked to be a female. A doe. Harvey noticed that the deer was missing her left front leg from the elbow down. It was not bleeding and seemed to be fully healed. He guessed that maybe it had been shot off during the previous hunting season. The deer survived though.

This reminded him of a time when he was thirteen and playing at Steve Tyson's house. All the kids were over at Steve's house and some girl was showing them how to use an Ouija board in the living room. Harvey had gone to the fridge to get an orange soda. Steve's dad was sitting at the table in a three piece suit looking at his whisky worriedly.

"How's your mama doing?" asked Steve's dad. Harvey's mother had been struggling with liver disease and was informed by the doctors that a transplant would be the only happy ending for her.

"She's doing well today, sir. She has good days and bad days," Harvey had said almost nervously. He had never known how to act around Steve's dad.

"Well, we're all hoping that she gets better. You may not understand it now, but one piece of advice I can give you for the future is that wounded creatures are sometimes the strongest," the distanced man mumbled.

The deer turned her head and looked directly at him. It seemed to him to have symbolic wisdom. He studied its head, its shape and the backdrop. He memorized it wholly in his mind and thought about his mother. He remembered how he never saw her taking a drink even though she always smelled like whisky.

A squirrel cracked a twig in a tree, startling the deer and it was gone just like that. Harvey exhausted himself from turning things over in his head. He went back into the cabin, turned the radio back on and sat down on the cold floor. He listened to music until darkness swallowed up into his consciousness and he fell asleep.

He would go back to Jenny Hastings the next day. The two would live the rest of their lives together. Harvey would never quite be able to mentally reconcile the concept that love could be both a weakness and a strength. Though he attempted quitting many times, Harvey would never be able to completely give up alcohol.

The End.

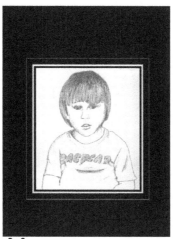

Randall C. Moss. What can be said about him that

hasn't already been said? Born from humble beginnings in Savannah, GA, he has since gone on to do great things such as read the back of a potato chip bag in its entirety and stare at a computer screen for nearly an hour and a half while trying to think of what to write about himself in the third person. You may wonder where he finds the time but, in addition he also works a full time job in sales where he exercises his story telling every time a coworker whips out a picture of their kid and asks him if they are cute (Sorry Sheila, that kid is ugly). I almost forgot to mention, every time he stubs his toe, he suddenly becomes multi-lingual. What can't this man do? In the future, he is hoping to up his attention span to the point where he can watch T.V. without looking at his phone. That has got to be close to the highest level of enlightenment! Good luck with that Mr. Moss!

Made in the USA
Monee, IL
17 December 2020